ANYONE SEEN HARRY LATELY?

ANYONE SEEN HARRY LATELY?

Hiawyn Oram ❖ Tony Ross

Andersen Press · London

Text copyright ©1988 by Hiawyn Oram. Illustrations copyright ©1988 by Tony Ross.
This paperback edition first published in 2001 by Andersen Press Ltd.
The rights of Hiawyn Oram and Tony Ross to be identified as the author and illustrator
of this work have been asserted by them in accordance with the Copyright, Designs and Patents Act, 1988.
First published in Great Britain in 1988 by Andersen Press Ltd., 20 Vauxhall Bridge Road, London SW1V 2SA.
Published in Australia by Random House Australia Pty., 20 Alfred Street, Milsons Point, Sydney, NSW 2061.
All rights reserved. Colour separated in Switzerland by Photolitho AG, Zurich.
Printed and bound in China.

10 9 8 7 6 5 4 3 2 1

British Library Cataloguing in Publication Data available.

ISBN 0 86264 198 5

This book has been printed on acid-free paper

Whenever Harry did not like
the way things looked,
he disappeared

re-appearing as some other Harry
for Harrysaurs are not required
to tidy rooms or hang up clothes,

Harrylions are never left
with babysitters half the night

and Harryfish are free to swim
and never told to wash their ears
because they have none.

So while others fought their battles face to face
Harry sailed behind some great disguises
and got away unscratched.

He thought, "Well, this is fun
and this is peaceful,"
and started doing it all the time
and couldn't stop himself

and then forgot himself.

His mother was the first to notice.
"Anyone seen Harry lately?
I went to tuck him up in bed
and found a *Harrygator*."

His father went next door to ask,
"Anyone seen Harry lately?"
The neighbours scratched their heads
and hummed, "A Harrybat was here last night—

but Harry—not for ages."
His friends came round and rang the bell.
His mother, pale and cross, peered out,
"Any of you seen Harry lately?"

A Harrytank zoomed down the stairs and
through the door and up the street.
His friends said, "Nice—but that's not him.
We've not seen Harry lately."

He sat unfed.
(No one feeds strange Harrystricters.)

He lay unkissed (no one kisses Harrybeetles)
and wondered where he'd lost himself
along the road to peace and quiet.

"I'd better have a search," he said
and called up all the characters
he'd used to wriggle out of things

and made them line up round the room
and stand there, marking time, all night.

But though he studied carefully
he couldn't see himself at all.
Or wait a minute . . . what was that . . .

the sudden narrowing of eyes . . .
the rudest little tongue pulled out.
"Ah ha," he said, "this looks like me . . ."
and urged his characters to worse.

"Go on. Let's see. Get more like me.
Refuse to do what you are told,
to be the things you're made to be."
Well, taking Harry at his word

and taking everything they'd need
those Harrycharacters made off
to find their own identity.

Still, good does come of bad, because
a Harry stripped of all disguises
quickly re-materialises.

"Yoo hoo," he yelled
and ran into his parents' room.
"Great news! Wake up! I'm back! It's me!"
His parents rolled and turned and stared.

"Who? Oh you! Have you tidied up your room?"
"Not yet," groaned Harry, "maybe later.
Besides it wasn't me who messed it.
I think it was that Harrygator."

"It really is our Harry back,"
his parents sighed
and let him in and held him tight
in case he disappeared again

but Harry said, "No chance of that.
Well, not tonight at any rate."